We Are Different!

Celebrating Differences

Emiliya King

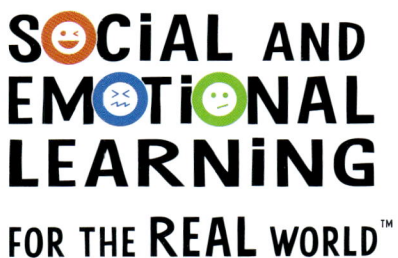

We come from different places.

We eat different foods.

We tell different stories.

We wear different clothes.

We use different words.

We are different.
But we are friends!

Words to Know

clothes

food

words